For Mary,

Pop! Pop!

Raine x

AuthorHouse™ UK Ltd.
500 Avebury Boulevard
Central Milton Keynes, MK9 2BE
www.authorhouse.co.uk
Phone: 08001974150

First published by AuthorHouse 2/16/2011

ISBN: 978-1-4567-7248-2 (sc)

Any people depicted in stock imagery provided by Thinkstock are models, and such images are being used for illustrative purposes only. Certain stock imagery © Thinkstock.

This book is printed on acid-free paper.

authorHOUSE®

R.H. For Fin, Tara, Jake, Aaron and Jack with love.

D.L. For my husband Mark with love.

Mother looked at her three little pigs.

A loud pop exploded followed by an even louder one.

"This is terrible," cried Mother, " my little boy is a popper."

His sisters could not stop laughing.

Mother told them not to be so rude.

She hoped he would grow out of it.

But he didn't.

As Pig grew he popped louder and louder and longer and longer.

One day he popped a thunder clap so loud that it blew their toilet through the wall and down the farm lane.

Pig was very upset and sad.
He went in search of a new home.

It was scary being on his own.
He popped a long loud one.
Mouse was so scared she ran away before Pig could say sorry.

Crossing the farmyard Pig met the Goat family.

"Please can I stay with you," he asked.

Father Goat said he needed help sweeping up leaves.

Pig was happy to help and worked very hard sweeping the leaves into a big pile.

Mother Goat brought out lunch.

Pig bent down to take some food.

And popped.

It was a real ripper and blew the leaves around the farmyard.

Not wanting a Pig that popped.

Father Goat asked him to leave.

Away he walked feeling very unhappy.

He wished he could find another home.

As Pig walked along he met Mother Hen and her little chicks.
"Please can I stay with you," he asked.
The chicks wanted him to stay.
Mother Hen agreed and Pig gave the chicks a ride on his back.

But before Pig could sit down he pop, pop, popped.

"Quick get down," shouted Mother Hen. "Someone is shooting at us with a machine gun."

"It was Pig. It was Pig," the chicks called out.

Not wanting a Pig that popped.

Mother Hen asked him to leave.

Pig walked away feeling very sad.

He wished he could find another home.

Tired and feeling very lonely he wandered into the stable.

Horse was settling down for the night and agreed that Pig could stay.

Pig found some straw and made himself a bed.

He was soon fast asleep.

Then it began, one pop, two pops, three.

By the time Horse counted to twenty he was stuffing straw into his ears to stop the noise.

Then Pig let off the longest pop he had ever popped.

It blew the stable door off its hinges.

Not wanting a Pig that popped.
Horse asked him to leave.
Pig walked away wishing he could stop popping.
Would he ever find another home.

Pig thought nobody loves me or wants me to live with them.
He sat down and cried.

Then he heard a loud noise coming from the farm pond.
He blew his nose, wiped his eyes and ran to see what it was.

The Ducks and Geese were having a fight.
"Why are you fighting," Pig shouted.

"We are the fastest swimmers on the pond," quacked the Ducks.
"No you are not, we are a lot faster than you," hissed the Geese.
They kept on fighting.
Pig yelled at the top of his voice, "STOP FIGHTING."

"Why don't you have a race and find out who really is the fastest,"
asked Pig.
The Ducks and Geese stopped fighting.
They agreed for the very first time.
A race was a very good idea.

The Ducks and Geese lined up at the edge of the pond.
Pig shouted, "Ready, Steady, Go," and off they raced.

At that very moment Pig let off the whopper of all pops.
He shot over the pond like a jet-propelled power boat.

The Ducks and Geese could not believe their eyes.
Pig had got there first and won the race.

Now there is peace in the farmyard.

All the animals heard about Pig and came to the pond to see him.
He gave the little animals rides on his back.
His sisters came and had rides too.
Everyone had such a good time.

The family told Pig how much they had missed him.
They built a new house beside the pond.

When Pig is not giving rides, he whizzes across the pond, popping
and popping, getting faster and faster.
He never feels unhappy now.

Pig is the happiest animal in the farm.

Lightning Source UK Ltd.
Milton Keynes UK
UKRC01n1938040918
328341UK00004B/33